May 2010
To Juliette—
   We've read this book many
times as you grew & grew!
   Now, you're big and it's time
to pass it on to you!
            Love—
                Grandma Pat

Library of Congress Cataloging-in-Publication Data Available

10 9 8 7 6 5 4 3 2 1

Published by Sterling Publishing Co., Inc.
387 Park Avenue South, New York, NY 10016
Text © 2004 by Harriet Ziefert
Originally published in 1989 by Viking Kestral
Illustrations © 2004 by Deborah Kogan Ray
Distributed in Canada by Sterling Publishing
c/o Canadian Manda Group, One Atlantic Avenue,
Suite 105, Toronto, Ontario, Canada M6K 3E7.
Distributed in Great Britain and Europe by Chris Lloyd at Orca Book
Services, Stanley House, Fleets Lane, Poole BH15 3AJ, England.
Distributed in Australia by Capricorn Link (Australia) Pty. Ltd.
P.O. Box 704, Windsor, NSW 2756, Australia.

Printed in China
All rights reserved
Sterling ISBN 1-4027-1703-2

P.S. Of course you will still
come & stay — but now you can
read to me! Love ya — G.G.

WITH LOVE FROM GRANDMA

Harriet Ziefert

PICTURES BY
Deborah Kogan Ray

Sterling Publishing Co., Inc.
New York

It was snowing outside—the first snow this winter—and it was even more special because Grandma was visiting us. Mama tucked me into bed. She pulled the blanket over me. Then Grandma spread a brightly colored afghan on top.

"It's so cold tonight," she said. "This will keep you extra warm, Katie."

The afghan was so nice. "Where did you get it?" I asked.

Grandma smiled. "There's a special story behind this afghan," she told me.

"Tell it!" I begged her.

This is the story she told . . .

My Nana—that would be your great-great-grandma—liked to keep busy. She cooked. She baked. She knitted. She knitted hats and gloves and mittens and socks and sweaters and scarves.

Nana loved to knit for her children and grandchildren. Everything she made was to keep us warm when winter came.

I visited my Nana every summer. I was her helper. We cooked and we baked. One day while we were waiting for a batch of cookies to cool, she said, "Sarah, I'm thinking of starting a big knitting project."

"What will you make?" I asked her. I hoped it would be something for me. A scarf, maybe.

"A scarf only takes a few hours to knit," Nana told me.

"What takes longer?" I asked her.

"An afghan!" she said.

The next morning we went to the store to buy wool. The shop was teeny tiny. The walls were lined with cubbyholes full of yarn in all the colors of the rainbow.

"I want skeins of your heaviest wool," Nana told the sales lady. And I got to pick the colors.

Orange was my favorite color, so I picked two different shades— one bright, and one lighter, like cantaloupe. Then I picked a green and a dark, dark red.

"Beautiful!" said Nana. "But we still need one more. How about this silver gray?"

Grandma pointed to the silver gray yarn in the afghan. "What do you think, Katie?"

"Perfect!" I said.

"I thought so too," said Grandma.

We left the knitting store with two big shopping bags. Nana carried one, and I carried the other. It was heavy! How many balls was I carrying anyway? I wanted to know.

"We bought six balls of each color," said Nana. "And we bought five different colors. So how many balls do we have altogether?"

I had just memorized my five-times table.

"Six times five equals thirty balls!" I told her. I was so proud.

By the time we got to Nana's apartment, my arm was aching, that bag was so heavy. Nana wanted to make lunch, but I didn't want to eat. I begged her to start the afghan right then.

Nana sat down on the sofa next to me. She took out a ball of orange wool and her afghan needles.

"I'm going to cast on thirty stitches," she said. "Then I'm going to knit back and forth, and back and forth, until I make a long strip of orange."

"How long?" I wanted to know.

"As long as your bed," she told me.

Nana knitted every day before lunch, and I watched the strip of orange grow longer and longer.

She tried to teach me by chanting, "Yarn over, go through two and pull one back; yarn over, go through two and pull one back." But I was more interested in roller skating.

Sometimes she stopped to count stitches. She said, "You have to make sure there are always thirty stitches on the needle. Otherwise the strips will be crooked."

Every day the strip got longer. Finally Nana decided it was long enough to take off the needle. She looked very pleased with herself.

"Watch me!" she said. "I'm casting off!"

When the last stitch was knotted and tied, Nana put down her needles and took out her crochet hook. She was going to crochet a border of green all around the strip. Then it would be finished.

I watched her loop the thread over and over again through the crochet hook until the border was finished. It looked so easy, I wanted to try it too. So Nana helped me crochet a bracelet, which I tied around my wrist.

"Do you still have the bracelet?" I asked Grandma.

She laughed. "I'm afraid I lost it long ago," she said. "But I can teach you to crochet a bracelet of your own if you like."

"Tomorrow?" I asked, and Grandma nodded.

When my vacation at Nana's was over, she took me to the bus station. She told the bus driver exactly where I was to get off and who was going to meet me. Then she kissed me good-bye and promised to call soon to let me know how the afghan was coming along.

School started. I called Nana to tell her I hardly had any time to practice crocheting because I was busy with school work and ballet. Nana told me that while I was busy with my homework, she was busy with my afghan. She had finished the green strip and crocheted a red border around it. Now she was working on a dark red strip.

I could hardly wait for Nana to come visit so I could see it.

Nana came to stay with me one weekend when my mother and father went away. She brought the two strips she had finished, and she was almost through with the red one.

As soon as she took the red strip off the needle and crocheted around it, she showed me what my afghan was going to look like. One by one, she carefully laid all the finished strips on my bed.

"My afghan—it's half done!" I shouted. "Three strips knitted and three strips to go!"

When it was time for Nana to leave, she rolled up the strips and stuffed them into her suitcase.

"I'll keep knitting," she promised when she kissed me good-bye. "The next time I come to visit, your afghan will be finished."

By then it was November and getting cold outside. I called Nana to tell her I was wearing the heavy red sweater she had knitted for me.

A few Sundays later, she called and said she was ready to bring the afghan.

"Don't hang up yet," my father said. He wanted to speak to Nana. He asked her to bring something for him—an apple pie. Daddy wanted a present too!

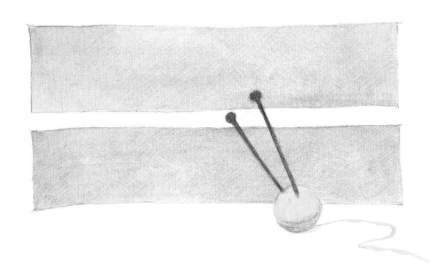

When Nana arrived with her bundles and bags, we were all happy to see her.

"Prepare the dining room table," she said. "I need a big clean surface."

My mother took the green felt pads out of the hall closet and covered the table with them. I helped. Nana put her knitting bag on top of the padded table. Out came six perfectly knitted strips—all with crocheted borders. But they were not sewn together.

I was disappointed. My afghan still was not finished.

"Don't be sad," said Nana. "We're going to sew the strips together right now. We'll have a sewing party!"

But I didn't know how to sew. I felt terrible.

"So I'll teach you—just like I taught you to crochet!" she said.

So my mother sewed. My father sewed. My Nana sewed. And I sewed! We sewed all the strips together.

That night Nana tucked me in. Then she covered me with the afghan.

At first I didn't notice, but then I saw that in one corner she had embroidered: *With love from Grandma — November 1955.*

Grandma showed me the spot.

"Wow!" I said. "That was a long time ago!"

Grandma laughed. "It sure was," she said. "That was before your mother was born!"

Then she finished her story.

Before I fell asleep I told Nana I would keep the afghan forever — even after I was grown up, and went to college, and got married.

"Afghans are forever," she said. "Someday you will give it to one of your children."

With Love
from Grandma
November
1955

"And now the afghan is yours," Grandma said. "A gift from your great-great grandmother to you. Goodnight, Katie."

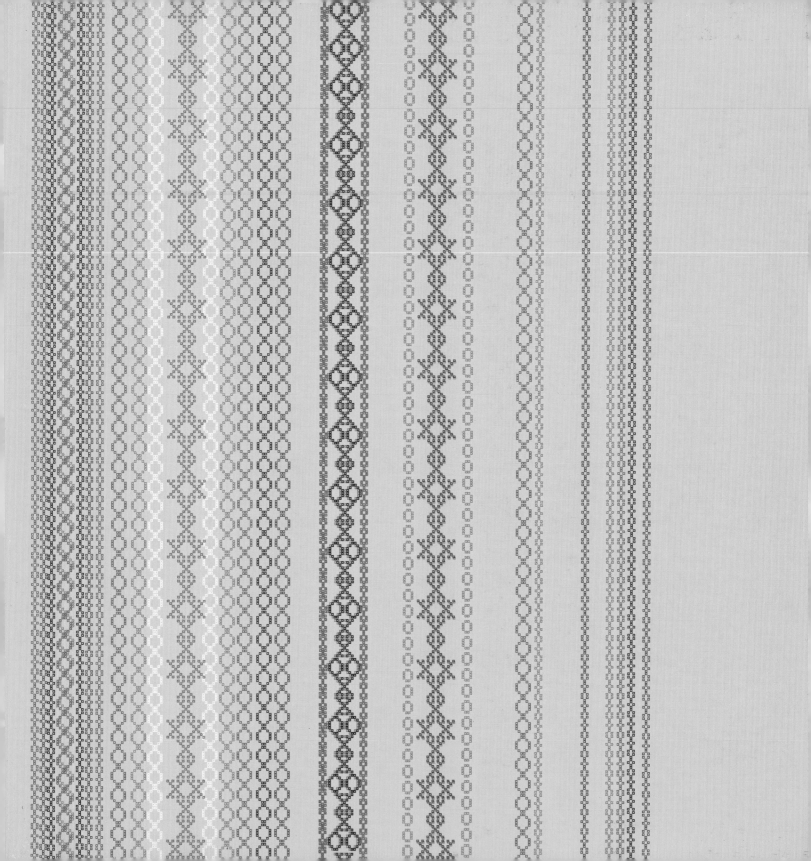